CW00841060

Young
Knight

BOOK BELONGS TO

....

The Big Biscuit

ANN PILLING

The Big Biscuit

illustrated by
Linda Birch

HODDER AND STOUGHTON

For my Thomas

British Library Cataloguing in Publication Data

Pilling, Ann
The big biscuit
I. II. Birch, Linda
823.914 [J]

ISBN 0-340-54734-0

First published 1989 by Hodder and Stoughton Children's Books
Young Knight edition first published 1991

Published by Hodder and Stoughton Children's Books,
a division of Hodder and Stoughton Ltd,
Mill Road, Dunton Green, Sevenoaks, Kent TN13 2YA

Printed in Great Britain by Cambus Litho, East Kilbride

Terence Bott was a fussy eater.

At breakfast he only ate his top layer of cornflakes. He said the bottom ones were too soggy.

At lunch he fed his peas and carrots to the dog.

At tea he just ate the middle bit of his sandwich. He hid the crusts down his jumper.

His favourite food was biscuits. He could eat biscuits all day long. One night his mother caught him eating them in bed.

'We'll get mice,' she said. 'And if you don't stop eating biscuits you'll turn into one.'

But Terence just laughed. He was munching peanut cookies under the covers.

Next morning he overslept.

'Wake up,' his mother said. 'You'll be late for school.'

Terence yawned, got up, and started to look round for his clothes. Then he stopped looking. He'd seen something very odd in his bedroom mirror.

It was a flat round yellow thing. It had Terence's hands and Terence's feet and Terence's face. But its front was covered with chocolate and its back was covered with sugar. Terence Bott had turned into a biscuit in the night.

'Hurry up!' shouted his mother.

So Terence struggled into his clothes. Now he was a biscuit they were all very tight. He walked down the stairs very slowly, in case his trousers ripped. At breakfast he ate every scrap. He wanted to get his mother into a good mood.

'I told you so,' she said, when she saw what had happened. 'Now get your coat on. We're late.'

Soon they were on their way to the bus stop. 'Can't you walk a bit quicker?' Mrs Bott complained.

Now he was a biscuit it was easier to roll along. So he did.

'Terence Bott, stand up this minute!' his mother yelled. 'We'll miss the bus.'

When it came, everyone climbed on.

'Full fare for biscuits!' the driver shouted. Terence was now so wide he took up a whole seat.

In the school playground they met Miss Green. 'I'm sorry, Mrs Bott,' she said. We don't take biscuits at Hill End Juniors.'

But Terence's mother was already going out through the gate. 'Be a good biscuit,' she told him.

Miss Green looked very cross. Then she saw a tear rolling down Terence's nose, and she took hold of his hand.

'Come along,' she said kindly. 'You can't stay out here all morning,' and she led Terence into his classroom.

Terence went and sat next to the radiator. He huddled up to it, hoping nobody would look at him. He might look like a biscuit but he still had human feelings. By playtime an awful thing had happened. Some of his chocolate had melted and there was a sticky puddle all over the floor.

Mr Moody the cleaner came with a mop.

'This is very careless,' he said.

Outside, all the children were eating their snacks. Terence hid behind the bike shed, but a greedy boy called Hugo Biggs pulled him out.

'Hey!' he shouted. 'Look what I've found. Anyone feeling hungry?'

They all crowded round. Some licked his chocolate off, some picked off his sugar, some started to take little bites. When playtime had finished, he wasn't round any more. He was frilled, like a pie-crust.

It was time to go home, before he got any smaller.

Soon it began to rain and puddles appeared on the pavements. Terence had to go very carefully now. If he fell into one he would turn into a soggy mess. He was already starting to crumble.

Near home he took a short cut, through the park. But it was a mistake. Everyone was out there, walking their dogs.

He started to run but it was too late.

Barking and yelping, they all chased after him. Their pink tongues hung out and their tails wagged. The had never seen such a big biscuit before. What did it taste like?

Terence got home just in time. He tore up the path, opened the door and slammed it behind him. Then he ran upstairs and shut himself in his room. Bed was the best place to hide. He climbed in and snuggled down. No one could take bites out of him up here.

But he was wrong. He woke up from a nice long sleep to find something nibbling at him, under the bedclothes.

Terence flung back the sheets and looked down. Sitting on his middle was a little brown mouse. He watched in horror as another came to join it. Then another. Then another.

You'll get mice if you eat biscuits in bed.

If only he'd listened to his mother. But it was too late.

All the mice in town must have heard about the big biscuit. They were crawling under the door and squeezing through the windows and climbing up on to Terence's bed to gobble him up.

By morning, there would be nothing left at all of Terence Arthur Bott.

He closed his eyes, opened his mouth, and screamed . . .

'Have you got a pain?' his mother said next morning. 'You were making an awful noise last night.'

'I had a horrible dream,' he answered. But he didn't dare look down. He might see a big biscuit lying there, in stripy pyjamas.

'Well it's time to get up. We're late again.' And she went off to put the kettle on.

His nightmare had made him very hungry. For breakfast he had two bowls of cornflakes, five slices of toast, and three glasses of milk. He wasn't a fussy eater any more.

Mrs Bott was amazed. 'Steady on,' she said. 'If you drink too much milk you'll turn into a cow. Promise me you'll be careful.'

Terence promised. He didn't want to turn into a cow.

Turning into a biscuit had been quite bad enough.

Other Young Knight titles you may enjoy: